HENRY'S AMAZING IMAGINATION!

NANCY CARLSON

VIKING

To Peter CARLSON,
Keep drawing AND using
Your "AMAZING" imagination !

♥ Aunt Nancy

VIKING
Published by Penguin Group
Penguin Young Readers Group, 345 Hudson Street, New York, New York 10014, U.S.A.
Penguin Group (Canada), 90 Eglinton Avenue East, Suite 700, Toronto, Ontario, Canada M4P 2Y3
(a division of Pearson Penguin Canada Inc.)
Penguin Books Ltd, 80 Strand, London WC2R 0RL, England
Penguin Ireland, 25 St Stephen's Green, Dublin 2, Ireland (a division of Penguin Books Ltd)
Penguin Group (Australia), 250 Camberwell Road, Camberwell, Victoria 3124, Australia
(a division of Pearson Australia Group Pty Ltd)
Penguin Books India Pvt Ltd, 11 Community Centre, Panchsheel Park, New Delhi – 110 017, India
Penguin Group (NZ), 67 Apollo Drive, Rosedale, North Shore 0632, New Zealand
(a division of Pearson New Zealand Ltd)
Penguin Books (South Africa) (Pty) Ltd, 24 Sturdee Avenue, Rosebank, Johannesburg 2196, South Africa

First published in 2008 by Viking, a division of Penguin Young Readers Group

1 3 5 7 9 10 8 6 4 2

LIBRARY OF CONGRESS CATALOGING-IN-PUBLICATION DATA
Carlson, Nancy L.
Henry's amazing imagination! / written and illustrated by Nancy Carlson.
p. cm.
Summary: When Henry's imagination gets mixed up with the truth during show and tell,
his teacher suggests that he write and illustrate his own stories.
ISBN 978-0-670-06296-6 (hardcover)
[1. Imagination—Fiction. 2. Show-and-tell presentations—Fiction.
3. Authorship—Fiction. 4. Kindergarten—Fiction. 5. Schools—Fiction.] I. Title.
PZ7.C21665Hdd 2008
[E]—dc22
2007031179

Manufactured in China
Set in Avenir
Book design by Sam Kim

Henry loved using his imagination . . .

especially during show and tell.

He told the class he caught a fish so big . . .

it pulled his boat across the whole lake!

And he built a snowman as big as his house.

Henry even told the class all about his
neighbor's pet, Joey.

The day Henry told them

an alien landed in his yard . . .

everyone started asking questions.

Tony said, "You're a big fibber!"

Henry didn't mean to fib . . . it's just that his imagination got mixed up with the truth.

After show and tell, Mr. McCarthy said,
"Henry, you have an amazing imagination.
Instead of using it for show and tell,

why don't you use it to write stories?"

"But . . . what if I can't spell all the words?"
"That's okay—just do your best!" said Mr. McCarthy.
"You can even draw pictures to go with them."

So Henry got busy at home . . .

and at school.

Now that Henry was using all his
imagination to write stories . . .

show and tell was really boring.

So boring Sydney fell asleep . . .

and Tony said, "I liked it better when you fibbed during show and tell."

But Henry knew he shouldn't fib . . .

so he got an idea.

At the next show and tell, Henry read his stories aloud. No one called him a fibber.

No one was bored. Everyone agreed: when Henry used his imagination to write stories . . .

show and tell was amazing!